MOJANG

MINECRAFT
WOODSWORD CHRONICLES

INTO THE GAME!

© 2019 Mojang AB and Mojang Synergies AB. MINECRAFT and MOJANG are trademarks or registered trademarks of Mojang Synergies AB. All rights reserved.

Published in the United States by Random House Children's Books, a division of Penguin Random House LLC, 1745 Broadway, New York, NY 10019, and in Canada by Penguin Random House Canada Limited, Toronto. Random House and the colophon are registered trademarks of Penguin Random House LLC.

rhcbooks.com
minecraft.net

Library of Congress Cataloging-in-Publication Data
Names: Eliopulos, Nick, author. | Flowers, Luke, illustrator.
Title: Into the game! / by Nick Eliopulos ; illustrated by Luke Flowers.
Description: New York : Random House, [2019] | Series: Woodsword Chronicles ; book 1
Identifiers: LCCN 2018051681 | ISBN 978-1-9848-5045-4 (hardback) | ISBN 978-1-9848-5046-1 (lib. bdg.) | ISBN 978-1-9848-5047-8 (ebook)
Subjects: | BISAC: JUVENILE FICTION / Media Tie-In. | JUVENILE FICTION / Action & Adventure / General.
Classification: LCC PZ7.E417 Int 2019 | DDC [Fic]—dc23

Cover jacket design by Diane Choi

Printed in the United States of America

20 19 18 17 16 15 14 13 12

MINECRAFT

WOODSWORD CHRONICLES

INTO THE GAME!

By Nick Eliopulos
Illustrated by Luke Flowers

Random House 🏠 New York

MORGAN

ASH

HARPER

PO

JODI

MS. MINERVA

DOC CULPEPPER

Prologue

HOW TO START A STORY WITH A CLIFFHANGER!

Four figures stood huddled around **a single torch**. It was the only source of light in the underground burrow. And they all knew that **monsters could not spawn in the light.**

"IT'S TOO CROWDED IN HERE," said one figure.

"WE CAN DIG DEEPER," said the second figure, who was holding a pickaxe. **"I COULD MAKE THE BURROW BIGGER."**

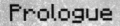

"NO, WE CAN'T RISK IT," said the third figure, who had crafted both the pickaxe and the torch. **"I DON'T HAVE**

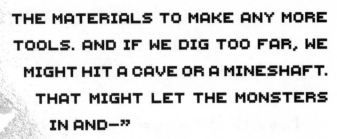

THE MATERIALS TO MAKE ANY MORE TOOLS. AND IF WE DIG TOO FAR, WE MIGHT HIT A CAVE OR A MINESHAFT. THAT MIGHT LET THE MONSTERS IN AND—"

The speakers went silent. They all heard it. Something out there was moaning. All four of them stood absolutely still.

After what seemed like forever, the moaning moved on. Everyone made eye contact. They nodded when they agreed it was gone.

"I WANT TO PINCH MYSELF TO SEE IF I'M DREAMING," one of them said, holding up a blocky hand, "BUT I DON'T HAVE ANY FINGERS HERE."

Here meant in Minecraft. As impossible as it seemed, the

four of them were inside their favorite video game. Really inside it. Living it. Minecraft was real.

That sounded like a good thing, but there was a problem:

They didn't know how to get back home to the real world.

Chapter 1

INTRODUCING ASH KAPOOR! NO ENEMY CAN DEFEAT HER! NO WALLS CAN KEEP HER AT BAY!

Ash Kapoor stood in the shadow of the castle. It was a cursed place, with dark windows and tall, twisting turrets. A flag snapped in the wind. On it was the image of some fearsome beast, the likes of which she'd never seen. A crow cawed in the distance.

Any other kid would be afraid right now, Ash thought. *But not me. I eat danger for breakfast!*

Ash had in fact eaten oatmeal for breakfast.

And she wasn't standing in front of a spooky old castle, either. It was just her new school, **Woodsword Middle**. But if she squinted at the building just right, she could imagine it was a

haunted fortress, or a forgotten temple, or an alien stronghold on some far-off moon.

Any of those places would be better than the truth: Ash was starting at another school as "the new kid" all over again. For the third time in three years, her family had been forced to move because of her mother's job.

She straightened her sash. It was part of her **Wildling Scout uniform,** and it displayed **dozens of badges. Each badge was a reminder** of something Ash had done well or a new skill she had mastered. They were like little trophies that stayed with her no matter how many times she had to start over. **She rubbed one for good luck.**

"You can't just stand in the middle of the staircase like that," said a boy as he stepped around her.

"Yeah, **are you lost** or something?" added a girl, who edged past Ash on the other side.

"Actually, I could use some directions!" said Ash. "I'm looking for room 247."

"It's right next to room 246," said the girl.

"And 248," said the boy. "You can't miss it."

Ash smiled pleasantly. "Thank you!" she said, although their "directions" had been far from helpful.

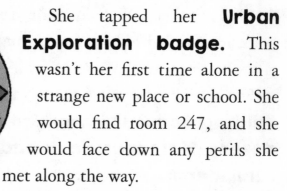 She tapped her **Urban Exploration badge.** This wasn't her first time alone in a strange new place or school. She would find room 247, and she would face down any perils she met along the way.

"Excuse me!" said another impatient voice at her back.

But first, she really had to stop standing in the middle of the staircase.

Ash was late when she reached room 247. She had hoped to slip in unnoticed. Instead, every single one of her classmates slid their eyes over to her as she walked in the door.

"Please take your seat," said the teacher,

shuffling through some papers on her desk.

"Um, I don't have a seat yet," said Ash. **"I'm new."**

"Oh! You're the new girl." The teacher looked up at her now. The woman's hair was frizzy. Her topknot was held back with knitting needles, as if it were a half-used ball of yarn. "I'm sorry, dear. **I'm so scatterbrained** before my first pot of coffee."

"Don't you mean your first *cup* of coffee?" asked Ash.

"I'm Ms. Minerva," she said, changing the subject. "Why don't you introduce yourself to the class?"

Ash turned toward her new classmates. She took a deep breath, tapping her **Public Speaking badge** for luck and putting on a bright smile. She had been through this before.

"Hi, everyone!" she said cheerfully. **"My name is Ash Kapoor.** I just moved here with my family from the West Coast, but I was born in Florida. I like scouting, animals, and **video games."**

A boy in the second row perked up. He pointed

to his binder, which was decorated with Minecraft stickers.

Ash nodded. "Minecraft especially," she added. Maybe she wouldn't have so much trouble making friends this time.

"An animal lover?" said Ms. Minerva. "Why, that gives me an idea. How would you like to take care of **Baron Sweetcheeks** for a while?"

The boy with the Minecraft binder perked up again. He raised his hand.

"Baron . . . Sweetcheeks?" Ash asked, uncertain.

"The class hamster," Ms. Minerva clarified. Then she whispered, "I didn't name him."

"Ms. Minerva?" the boy said, waving his hand.

"Yes, Morgan?"

The boy straightened up in his seat. "Baron Sweetcheeks is actually a lot of work."

Ms. Minerva sighed. "Twenty-four children are a lot of work, Morgan. **Baron Sweetcheeks is a hamster."**

"Sure, he looks cute," Morgan Mercado said. "From a distance! But if you neglect him even a

little bit, he **freaks out.** He needs food, fresh water, exercise, cute hats, intellectual stimulation—"

"It sounds like you could use a break from the hamster, Morgan," said their teacher.

Morgan shook his head. "No, I—"

"I don't mind," Ash said. "I'm happy to help. I'll start today."

"It's settled, then," said Ms. Minerva. "Ash, there's an open seat in the back there."

Ash felt quite happy. The day was off to a good start. And she had so much in common with Morgan! As she walked past him on the way to her seat, she gave him a friendly little wave.

He didn't wave back.

Chapter 2

HYPOTHESIS: OUR SCIENCE TEACHER IS FROM A POST-APOCALYPTIC FUTURE

Jodi Mercado looked over her list of equipment. Binoculars: check. Sunglasses: check. Trench coat: too hot and probably not necessary, so she had left it at home.

She had done her research. She knew all the tools of the **spy trade.**

"It's difficult to use sunglasses and binoculars at the same time, though," she said, switching back and forth between the two.

"Excuse me," said a voice at Jodi's back. She turned and saw the new girl standing there. "Is this second-period gym?"

"Yes," Jodi replied quickly. "Welcome! Here, hold these, please." She handed her sunglasses over. The binoculars gave a much clearer view. She now saw her **science teacher, Doc Culpepper,** walking through the school parking lot with a box full of circuit boards and wires and . . . gadgets of some sort.

"Sorry, one more question," said the new girl. "Where is the gym teacher?"

"Coach Graham is always three or four minutes late," Jodi answered. "Which means these are the best three minutes of the day to test my hypothesis."

"Hypothesis?" echoed the new girl.

"It means an educated guess," explained Jodi. "You try to prove your guess is right or wrong through experimentation or observation."

"I know what a hypothesis is," the girl replied. "We already had our science fair at my last school. I meant, what is your hypothesis?"

"I think our science teacher is from the future," Jodi answered. "I think she was fighting evil robots, but the robots were winning. So she traveled back to our time to change the past and prevent them from conquering the world."

The new girl laughed. But it wasn't a mean laugh. Jodi knew what a mean laugh sounded like.

Jodi lowered her binoculars and continued. "Culpepper is new this year. She's brilliant. She's a real doctor! I looked her up online, and she has worked on artificial intelligence. So what is she doing at our school?"

"Maybe she enjoys teaching," said the new girl.

"That's an interesting hypothesis," said Jodi. "But I like mine better."

"Well, I have bad news," said the girl. "I think your science project has gotten away."

Jodi spun around and looked through the binoculars. "How did she do that?" she asked. "Did she step through **a time portal?**"

"She stepped into . . . **a minivan!**" the new girl answered dramatically.

"Hmmm . . . ," said Jodi, disappointed. "That's so normal, **it's almost suspicious. . . .**"

The new girl giggled. "I'm Ash, by the way."

Jodi put the binoculars away. "I'm Jodi. I saw you this morning. We both have Ms. Minerva for homeroom." She pointed to Ash's sash. "So you're a Wildling Scout? **You have so many badges!**"

Ash nodded. "Unfortunately, there's no **Spycraft badge.** But maybe I can help you anyway. I do have a badge for bird-watching. And camouflage. And drone building."

"Oh, I love the drone idea," Jodi said. "I could

paint it to look like **a ghast!**" She scratched her chin. "But what if Doc takes control of it remotely with **advanced technology** from the twenty-third century?"

"You're right," said Ash. "A drone is too risky."

Jodi sighed. "I need **a real science**

project, anyway." She perked up. "Wait. Did you say you've already done one this year?"

"Yes," Ash said. She pointed to a badge with the image of a test tube on it. "**I made an exploding piñata.** It uses carbon dioxide."

"A piñata you don't even have to hit?" Jodi said. "It's the invention of the century!"

"The **science is easy,**" said Ash. "But it takes an artist to make it look like a real piñata."

Jodi grinned from ear to ear. "You want to be partners? You bring the science, I'll bring the art."

Ash smiled back. "Sure."

A shrill whistle cut through the air.

"Our three minutes are up," Jodi said. "Follow me!"

Jodi was a year younger than the other kids. The teachers all said she had "creative problem-solving skills." That seemed to be a polite way to say that she was smart but impulsive—both traits shared by all the members of the Mercado family. But where her brother usually tried to control himself and look cool in front of their classmates (she didn't think he was all that successful), **Jodi liked to follow her artistic whims,** no matter what anyone thought.

Her "creative problem-solving" made her seem a little odd, but **there was no denying that**

she was smart. She had been allowed to skip a grade. That was why she was in the same classes as her older brother, Morgan.

In most cases, being younger than her classmates wasn't a big deal. But she always felt the difference in gym. She was just a little bit shorter than

everyone else. It put her at a disadvantage for most sports.

So she'd made a deal with Morgan. **They called it their pact.** When it was his turn to choose teams, he would always choose her first. And when it was Jodi's turn, she would choose Morgan first. That way, they were always on the same team.

Morgan was **a good big brother.** So good that she was reluctant to do what she was about to do: she was going to break their pact. She only hoped Morgan would understand.

It was Jodi's turn to choose. And Ash looked so hopeful, standing on her tiptoes and waving. Jodi realized that she was probably one of the only people Ash knew in the entire school.

"Go ahead, Jodi," said Coach Graham. "Make your first pick."

Morgan took a step forward.

"I choose Ash," Jodi said quickly, before she could change her mind.

Ash looked so happy. She rushed to Jodi's side. "Thanks," she whispered.

Jodi felt warmth in her chest. She was sure **she'd done the right thing.** And she was sure Morgan would understand.

She glanced across the asphalt at her brother.

Uh-oh. Maybe he wouldn't.

Chapter 3

SCIENCE! WITHOUT IT, THERE WOULD BE NO CANDY

Several days later, Harper Houston stepped back to admire her team's creation. She smiled.

There was just something beautiful about a perfectly constructed volcano.

"I hope this works," said Po Chen. He was one of her partners for the science fair.

"It will work," Harper promised. **"That's the beauty of science.** If you follow the instructions, you get the same result every time." She turned to Morgan, the third member of their group. "Right, Morgan?"

Morgan didn't say anything.

"Right, Morgan?" she repeated.

But Morgan wasn't paying attention to her. He was looking toward the doors of the auditorium. Harper turned to look, too. She saw Morgan's sister, Jodi, with the new girl, Ash. **They were arriving with their own project.** It was tall and covered with a white sheet, like a Halloween costume of a ghost.

"What is that?" Harper asked him. "Did your sister make a volcano, too?"

"I don't know," Morgan answered. "They've been working on it **in secret** for days."

"Well, don't let it distract you," Harper said. "This isn't a competition."

He raised an eyebrow at her. "They hand out trophies for the best projects. I'm pretty sure that makes it a competition."

Harper sighed. She just didn't worry about things like that. **She loved learning for the sake of learning**—especially science. And she didn't need a trophy to know that her team had done a good job.

There were other volcanoes made of paper-mache, clay, and other craft materials in the auditorium. But none of them was quite like theirs. They had constructed it out of **one hundred identically sized cubes** of modeling clay. It was brown and green and blocky. And it looked like something right out of Minecraft.

Harper, Morgan, and Po were very different. **But they all liked Minecraft.** That had been all the inspiration they needed.

Po pulled the finishing touches from his backpack: a bottle of vinegar and a box of baking soda. A small amount of each would make their volcano erupt. That would prove to the teachers that they understood chemical reactions. **And a dash of red food coloring would give it some flair!**

"What do you think their project is?" Morgan asked. Jodi and Ash were setting up their station nearby. Morgan couldn't take his eyes off them.

"Focus, Morgan," Harper said in a singsong voice. "Do you have the food coloring?"

"Yeah," Morgan grumbled. He began rooting around in his backpack.

Just then, Ash and Jodi pulled their sheet

away with a flourish. **Their project wasn't a volcano.** They had constructed a piñata. It looked just like a **MINECRAFT CREEPER,** with a green body and black eyes. It was as tall as Jodi.

Kids *oohed* and *aahed*. Harper couldn't blame them. The creeper looked amazing.

Morgan went pale. **"But ... but ...,"** he said. "Minecraft is my thing."

Ash saw him looking. She smiled and waved.

Morgan didn't wave back.

"You don't own Minecraft," Po reminded him. **"But they copied our idea!"** Morgan said.

"It's probably a coincidence," Harper said.

Ms. Minerva and Doc Culpepper looked the piñata over. They smiled and nodded and wrote notes on their clipboards. Then Ash directed the teachers and students to step back to a safe distance. **Ash put on a pair of safety goggles.** She attached a hose to the back of the piñata, and then she joined the other students.

At the other end of the hose, Jodi stood beside a canister of gas. **It was labeled CO_2.** Harper recognized that as the chemical formula for carbon dioxide. *I wonder what they're up to?* she thought, her mind racing with possibilities.

At a signal from Ash, Jodi turned a handle on the CO_2 tank. The hose went taut as gas moved from the tank to the piñata.

Harper held her breath, excited to see what would happen next.

The creeper exploded! It was just like in Minecraft. Except when this creeper exploded, it sent candy flying across the floor.

"Amazing," Harper said. "They made a piñata that breaks itself."

All the other children cheered and laughed as **they ran forward to grab fistfuls of candy.** Doc Culpepper

cheered, and Ms. Minerva gave Jodi and Ash a thumbs-up.

"That does it," Morgan said. "We need to go bigger."

"Bigger?" Po asked.

"Our volcano is measly compared to that. **We need a much bigger eruption!**"

Harper shook her head. "That's a terrible

idea, Morgan. Our volcano will work just fine if we stick to the plan." She picked up her measuring spoons and poured out a tablespoon of vinegar.

But Morgan took the bottle from her and the box of baking soda from Po. He held everything out over the mouth of the volcano.

"Morgan, wait!" Po said.

Harper added, "We don't know what will happen if you—"

But once more, Morgan wasn't listening. He dumped everything into the volcano.

At first, nothing happened. Then the volcano began to rumble. And shake. And then—

A blast of red liquid burst forth, spraying the whole auditorium. **Students screamed and scattered.** They dropped their precious candy as they fled. Ms. Minerva stood frozen in shock as red foam dripped from her hair. Her clipboard was ruined.

"Oops," said Morgan.

Harper slapped her forehead in disbelief.

Chapter 4

SURVIVAL MODE +
UNTESTED VR GOGGLES =
IT'S PROBABLY SAFE...
RIGHT?

Po wasn't used to getting into trouble. Of course, he also never drenched his entire class in foul-smelling red foam. Today was a day of firsts.

Ms. Minerva had sent everyone to wash up. Only Harper, Morgan, and Po remained in the auditorium. Po hoped they wouldn't be punished too severely. They'd made a big mess, but baking powder and vinegar wasn't dangerous.

Then Ms. Minerva said the words that Po most

dreaded hearing: "I'm very disappointed in you," she said. "All of you."

Those words cut Po deep. He didn't like to disappoint anyone. Ever.

He looked at Harper. Her eyes were ablaze. Those eyes seemed to say **"It was all Morgan's fault."** They also seemed to say "But I can't say that without sounding like a snitch." And finally, her eyes added "Morgan, now is where you speak up and take responsibility for your actions. Now. Right . . . now."

Harper had very expressive eyes.

Morgan did speak up. But he didn't confess. **"Why are we in trouble?"** he asked. "The volcano did what it was supposed to do. The eruption was just a little bigger than expected."

Ms. Minerva shook her head. Po squirmed in his wheelchair. There was a squelching sound from the "lava" beneath him.

A voice sounded at their backs. "Don't be too hard on them, Minerva." Po pivoted to see that **Doc Culpepper** had joined them. "After all, no scientist ever achieved anything by being too

cautious."

"That's definitely not true," Ms. Minerva said.

Culpepper shrugged. "Anyway, I could use the help of a few daring researchers on a science project of my own."

Harper grinned from ear to ear. Po knew that she idolized Doc.

"What are you all doing after school today?" Doc asked brightly.

Ms. Minerva rolled her eyes and quickly replied, "They're mopping the auditorium!"

"Ah, right," said Doc. "What about after that? Do you have time to come by **the computer lab?**"

Harper and Morgan both agreed eagerly. Po hesitated for a moment. He was supposed to go to basketball practice. He could probably use it as an excuse to avoid whatever Doc Culpepper had in mind for them. He could probably even get out of mopping with Morgan and Harper. But that didn't seem fair to his friends.

"I'll be there," he said.

When Po arrived at the computer lab later that day, Harper and Morgan were already there. So was Morgan's sister, Jodi.

"Hey, Jodi," Po said. "Nice job on **the creeper.** Why are you here with the detention club?"

"I can't walk home without my big brother," Jodi said.

"**This isn't detention**," Morgan corrected him.

"Right," Harper said. "Doc said she was impressed with us. She actually wants our help. I wonder what her project is."

Jodi grinned. "As long as it doesn't involve **evil robots** from the twenty-third century."

"Don't be so pessimistic, young lady," said Doc as she entered the room. "We'll have evil robots long before the twenty-third century."

Jodi's eyes went wide. She looked around to see if anyone had caught how ominous that sounded.

"I'll get right to the point, kids," said Doc. "As you know, I'm something of **an amateur inventor**."

Po did know that. He also knew that Doc's inventions tended to cause more problems than they solved. After her so-called improvements to the school's dance and drama club spotlights, the cast of *The Nutcracker* had seen spots for weeks. And the latte machine she'd installed in the teachers' lounge had brewed **coffee so strong it had kept all the teachers awake for three days** and nights. Only Ms. Minerva had been unaffected.

"This time," Doc promised, "I've got something really special." She held up a pair of goggles.

Harper squinted. "Are those **VR goggles?**"

Doc smiled. "That's right! Virtual reality makes digital spaces seem real. Mostly it's used for **video games.** But I think soon we'll be doing our online shopping in virtual malls. Maybe even attending school virtually."

Po gasped. "But without school . . . there would be no Taco Tuesday!"

Jodi patted him on the shoulder. "There could be virtual **Taco Tuesdays.**"

"It wouldn't be the same," he said, pretending to wipe away a tear.

Doc cleared her throat to get their attention.

"I've made **some improvements** to the standard VR goggles. I think. But I need volunteers to test them out."

"Let me get this straight," said Morgan. **"you want us to stay after school to play video games?** I'd say I must be dreaming, but I can still smell the vinegar on my clothes."

Doc gave them each a set of goggles. They were heavier than they looked. Wires stuck out of them. And they were covered in strange, glowing blue symbols.

"What do the symbols mean?" Harper asked.

"They're just decoration," Doc said.

"Would these work on Minecraft?" Po asked.

"I think that's a great idea," said Doc. "You're all so familiar with that game, you'd know if something was different about it. **You'd notice if the goggles changed the game somehow.** Just give me a minute to set up a network so that you're all playing on the same server."

Po watched in awe as Doc lifted a PC tower onto a central table. It looked as if it had been cobbled together from a dozen scrapped computers. Its internal workings were exposed here and there because the pieces didn't fit together perfectly. Po could see a motherboard, **an impossible tangle of wires,** and more memory cards than he thought a computer could hold.

"It's the Frankenstein of computers," said Po.

"It's beautiful," Harper added. "What sort of

processor are you running on that thing?"

"I had to build my own," Doc said with a wink. "Give me a hand?"

While Harper flitted about the jigsaw computer, Po adjusted his goggles so that they sat on his forehead. He felt a thrill of anticipation.

The computer booted up. Multiple fans began to whir. Doc typed some commands into a keyboard. "That should do it," she said. Then, in a tone that Po found strangely serious, she said, **"Good luck, kids."**

Morgan turned to the others. **"Survival mode or Creative?"** he asked.

Jodi said, "Creative," but both Po and Harper voted for Survival.

"Survival it is," Morgan said. "Everybody get ready."

Po's mouth had gone dry. He licked his lips, then **slipped the goggles down over his eyes.** Instead of the computer lab, he saw a familiar game menu. He'd seen it a hundred times before, but now it took up his entire field of vision.

Morgan selected Survival mode.

There was a bright flash of light. Po closed his eyes.

And when he opened them again, what he saw took his breath away.

Generating World
Building terrain

Chapter 5

MINECRAFT—LIVE IN 3...2...1...!!!

Like Po, Morgan couldn't believe what he was seeing. He shook his head. He blinked rapidly. He rubbed his eyes . . . **with blocky brown hands.**

It wasn't just his hands that were blocky. The trees were stacks of brown and green cubes. The sun was a yellow square in the bright blue sky.

"WE'RE INSIDE THE GAME," he said. **"WE'RE INSIDE MINECRAFT."**

It sounded impossible. But Harper said, **"YEAH. I THINK WE ARE."**

Po said, **"YOU'RE RIGHT."**

And Jodi said, **"WA-HOO!"**

Jodi bounded down a hill, whooping with delight all the way to the bottom.

Morgan watched her go. She was definitely his sister. But she looked different. Like a video-game avatar of herself.

He turned to look at the others. **They looked like avatars, too.** They were blocky and pixelated but still instantly recognizable. They wore clothes similar to what they'd been wearing

back in the computer lab.

"I've played some games in VR before," Harper said. **"THIS IS DIFFERENT."**

"IT SURE IS," Po said. "I don't hear Doc's computer fans whirring, do you?" He touched his face. **"I DON'T FEEL THE GOGGLES. OR MY WHEELCHAIR.** But I can feel the ground and the sunlight." He jumped up and down. He grinned. **"WE'RE NOT JUST SEEING THIS. IT'S LIKE WE'RE REALLY HERE."**

"Maybe," Harper said. "The brain is a mysterious organ. Scientists don't fully understand how it works. What if Doc's goggles are tricking our brains and making us think we're here? It could all be an elaborate illusion."

"LIKE A DREAM?" Morgan asked. **"A DREAM THAT WE'RE ALL EXPERIENCING TOGETHER?"**

"That's as good a hypothesis as any," Harper said. "Maybe we can come up with an experiment to test it."

"NO, THANK YOU!" Po said brightly. **"IF YOU REMEMBER, OUR LAST SCIENCE**

EXPERIMENT DIDN'T GO SO WELL. Why don't we just enjoy ourselves?"

With that, Po was off, speeding to the bottom of the hill, where Jodi was running around in circles.

Harper walked over to a tree. She hit its trunk several times. Each time, little chips of wood flew into the air, until finally, a whole piece of the trunk broke off.

Morgan flinched. **In the real world, gravity would cause the tree to crash to the ground.** But here, just as in the game, it remained standing even with a piece of its trunk missing.

Harper picked up the chunk of wood that she'd hacked off the tree. At her touch, it disappeared with a popping sound.

"WHERE'D IT GO?" said Morgan.

"GOOD QUESTION," said Harper.

She moved her hands around in the air. She made strange expressions with her face.

"ARE YOU OKAY?"

"I'm trying to figure out— Aha!" she cried. **"IF YOU BLINK TWICE QUICKLY—LIKE DOUBLE-CLICKING A COMPUTER MOUSE— YOUR INVENTORY COMES UP!"**

"THAT'S TOO WEIRD," Morgan said. But he decided to give it a try. He double-clicked his eyes. Sure enough, an inventory menu popped up, blocking his view of Harper. It looked a little bit like an empty, floating bookshelf.

Morgan also saw a row of hearts and a row of food. **"WE HAVE HEALTH AND HUNGER METERS, TOO,"** he said. He double-clicked his eyes again, and the interface disappeared.

"I WANT TO TRY SOMETHING," said Harper. Morgan watched as her eyes and fingers moved around. **"I HAVE A PIECE OF OAK,"** she said. **"IF I CAN USE THAT TO MAKE FOUR PLANKS..."**

She closed her eyes. Suddenly, there was a *clunk,* and a table appeared in front of her.

It was a crafting table.

"HARPER!" Morgan cried. **"THAT'S INCREDIBLE."**

Harper grinned. **"I'M NOT DONE YET."** She broke off more of the tree. "Now I have two pieces of oak. Each one makes four planks, so . . ." She closed her eyes. There was another *clunk.* **"I HAVE EIGHT PLANKS. I'LL USE ONE OF THEM TO MAKE A BATCH OF STICKS, AND THEN, IF I USE THE CRAFTING TABLE . . ."**

Morgan saw the moment it happened. Harper flexed her hand a little, and a wooden pickaxe appeared out of nowhere.

Well, not exactly out of nowhere, Morgan realized. She had crafted it from the materials she'd taken from the tree.

Now Morgan was really excited. **Really being inside a video game was cool.** And being inside a video game where he could make almost anything he could imagine was even cooler.

He just hoped he remembered some recipes. He didn't have his guidebooks here.

Morgan started punching the environment to fill his inventory. He got **oak, dirt, and some seeds** from tall grass. It was all basic stuff. But he knew that it might come in handy.

He looked over to see Harper marveling at the floating tree. **"THIS JUST FEELS SO REAL,"** she said.

Po was chasing a flock of sheep. Jodi was building a sphinx-like statue out of dirt blocks.

As the afternoon progressed, the sun sank lower in the sky. Morgan thought they should probably be getting home. **"HEY,"** he said. **"THAT INVENTORY VIEW DIDN'T HAVE ANYTHING ABOUT DISCONNECTING, DID IT?"**

Harper turned away from her tree. **"NO,"** she said. **"I HAVEN'T BEEN ABLE TO FIND ANY SORT OF MENU."**

Morgan touched his face. He still couldn't feel the VR goggles. He couldn't feel any part of his real body back in the real world.

"HOW DO WE EXIT?" he asked.

Harper thought about it for a moment. **"THAT IS AN EXCELLENT QUESTION,"** she said at last.

"We need to figure it out." He looked again at the sky and the lowering sun. **"BUT FIRST, WE SHOULD FIND SHELTER."**

"Why?" she asked. **"WE JUST GOT HERE. WE SHOULD EXPLORE!"**

"But it's going to be night soon," said Morgan. "And when we started the game . . ."

"OH. RIGHT," said Harper. **"WE SET IT TO SURVIVAL MODE."**

Finding shelter was easy. Harper used her pickaxe to dig into the hill. She kept digging until she'd made **a cavelike hole** large enough for all of them to fit inside.

Before they could close off the entrance with dirt, they would need a way to make light. No

one wanted to be trapped underground in total darkness.

"WE COULD DIG FOR COAL," suggested Po.

"That sounds risky," Morgan said. **"THE MORE WE DIG, THE MORE LIKELY WE ARE TO FIND A MINESHAFT."**

"Is that a bad thing?" asked Jodi.

"IT IS IF IT'S FULL OF HOSTILE MOBS,"

Morgan answered.

Harper had an idea. **"MORGAN, I SAW YOU PICKING UP THE COBBLESTONE I DUG THROUGH EARLIER. DO YOU HAVE AT LEAST EIGHT BLOCKS?"**

Morgan closed his eyes. He saw everything he'd picked up so far in his inventory. He had twelve blocks of cobblestone.

"YES," he said.

"THAT'S ENOUGH TO MAKE A FURNACE," Harper said. "And with a furnace, and some wood to burn . . ."

"WE CAN MAKE CHARCOAL," Morgan finished. **"AND THEN A TORCH! LET'S DO IT."**

It was now fully dark outside. In the distance, Morgan heard the unmistakable groan of a zombie.

"AND LET'S DO IT FAST," he said.

Chapter 6

COUNTING SHEEP:
CURE FOR INSOMNIA!
FUN GROUP ACTIVITY!

Jodi was the first one to step out into the night.

All was silent. The only sources of illumination were the moon above and Morgan's torch behind her. The pixilated moon was cold and eerie. But the light of the torch was warm and soft.

She listened for the sounds of creatures. She watched for any movement beyond the torchlight.

"IT'S ALL

CLEAR," she whispered. **"LET'S GO."**

They had come up with a plan while huddled in their burrow. Whenever any of them were ready to quit a game, they would go to sleep in a bed. It was how they would set **a new respawn point.** Morgan thought it might be the closest thing they had to "disconnecting."

They weren't sure it would work. But it was the best plan they had.

To make a bed, however, **they would need**

wool. To get wool without hurting the sheep, they would need shears. To make shears, they needed iron. Which meant **digging deeper** into the burrow. Exactly what Morgan had warned them not to do.

But they got lucky: they found iron ore before they found anything dangerous. To mine it, **Harper upgraded her pickaxe** from wood to stone.

That was how Survival mode worked, Harper explained to Jodi. Getting stuff to make stuff to get better stuff. And hoping you didn't run into any monsters while you were unprepared.

It set Jodi's nerves on edge. **"I JUST WANT TO REMIND EVERYONE THAT I VOTED FOR CREATIVE MODE,"** she whispered.

At least they were on the final stage of their plan. They only had to get back to the sheep they had seen earlier in the day.

It was a short walk to the clearing where they had first spawned. But when they got there . . .

"NO SHEEP," said Morgan.

"BAA, HUMBUG," Jodi said. **"GET IT?**

BAAAA—"

"Maybe we should wait until morning?" Po suggested.

"I don't think we can afford to wait," Harper said. **"I'M GETTING HUNGRY. ANYBODY ELSE?"**

The others nodded. Jodi realized she was hungry, too.

"I see what you mean," Morgan said. **"IF HUNGER WORKS HERE LIKE IT DOES IN THE GAME . . ."**

"THEN WE'LL START LOSING HEALTH SOON," Harper finished.

"That doesn't sound good," Po said.

"We know how the game works, at least," Morgan said. "If we really are stuck here, we can hunt for food and build a better shelter."

"Let's call that plan B," said Po. **"I STILL WANT TO TRY THE BED THING."**

Morgan nodded. "Jodi's bleating gave me an idea. Let's be quiet for a minute."

Whenever Morgan told her to be quiet, Jodi liked to do the opposite. But just this once, she decided to go along with him.

She was glad she did. They stood in silence for only a few seconds before they heard sounds in the distance.

"THOSE ARE SHEEP!" Jodi said. **"THIS WAY."**

Jodi hurried forward across the grass. The others were right behind her. They all paused when the plain ended at a line of trees.

"IT'S DARKER IN THERE," Morgan whispered, lifting his torch.

Sheep bleated just beyond the trees.

"WE HAVE TO BE BRAVE," said Jodi. Her voice quavered a little. She didn't sound convinced. **It was definitely scarier being here in person than it was watching it all on a screen.**

They passed through the trees. Luckily, they found that it wasn't a full forest, only a small grove. They quickly reached the other side. The sheep were grazing in a clearing.

Harper pulled out her shears and handed them to Jodi.

"YOU'LL HAVE TO BE QUICK," Harper said. **"DON'T LET THEM GET AWAY."**

"You're right," Jodi said. "Just this once, running with scissors is a good idea."

Jodi managed to get three tufts of wool before the sheep escaped through the trees. It was only enough to make a single bed.

Back at the burrow, Harper arranged the wool

and wood planks in the proper sequence. There was a *clunk,* and suddenly a bed stood in the middle of the room.

"ALL RIGHT," Harper said. "WHO'S FIRST?"

"Jodi's the youngest," Morgan said. "She should go first."

"WHAT DOES MY AGE HAVE TO DO WITH ANYTHING?" Jodi said crossly.

"SHHH!" said Po.

The moaning sound was back. It was closer than before.

"NO ARGUMENTS, JODI," Morgan said. "YOU GO FIRST."

"All right," Jodi said. She stepped toward the bed. "BUT IF YOU EXPECT ME TO BE ABLE TO SLEEP WITH ALL THAT MOANING—"

Before she could finish the thought, everything went dark. Jodi felt the weight of the goggles on her face.

She quickly removed the goggles. **She was back in the computer lab back in the**

real world.

She looked around. Morgan, Harper, and Po were all wearing their goggles and sitting completely still. She poked Morgan, then pinched him. Nothing happened. It was as if his mind was elsewhere. But anyone watching would just think he was very interested in the game.

There were sharp whispers coming from the corner of the room, and Jodi turned to see Ms. Minerva and Doc Culpepper. Although they kept their voices down, they were waving their arms and wagging their eyebrows. It looked like they were having an argument.

Ms. Minerva saw Jodi watching them. A huge smile broke out on her face. "Jodi," she said.

"Ms. Minerva!" Jodi said. **"Doc! The game— it's real. We were really inside Minecraft!"**

Doc chuckled. "Yes, virtual reality can certainly seem real."

Jodi shook her head. "You don't understand. It was . . . We were—"

"We really enjoyed it," Morgan said. "Doc Culpepper, **your VR goggles work perfectly."**

Jodi turned around. Morgan was standing at her shoulder.

He winked at her, as if to say *Trust me.*

"You didn't notice anything unexpected?" Ms. Minerva asked. **"Doc's inventions are sometimes ... strange."**

"No, ma'am," Morgan said. "It was a normal game of Minecraft. Just a little more realistic, that's all."

A little? thought Jodi.

"You see, Minerva?" said Doc. "There was nothing to worry about."

Ms. Minerva looked unsure.

"Do you . . . think we could use them again sometime?" Morgan asked.

Jodi couldn't believe her ears. "You want to go through that again?" she asked him.

"I hope you will," said Doc. "I need a thorough list of any glitches you find. Anything that seems strange or broken. Until the project is complete, I'm leaving all six pairs of goggles in your care."

"Awesome!" Morgan said.

Both teachers gave him a look.

"I mean . . . you can trust us to be responsible with them," Morgan said.

"That's better," said Ms. Minerva.

Jodi saw that Harper had removed her goggles and was rubbing her eyes. Po was moving, too.

She pulled her brother aside. **"What are you doing?"** she asked.

"What are *you* doing?" he demanded. "That was amazing. If the adults think it was dangerous, they'll take it away."

"It was dangerous," Jodi said. "Five minutes ago, I thought we were going to be **eaten by a zombie.**"

"Zombies aren't that dangerous if you know how to handle them," Morgan said. "We were just unprepared. Next time, we'll be ready."

Jodi frowned. "Zombies aren't that dangerous" **sounded like famous last words.**

Morgan turned to Harper and Po. "So. Want to meet back here after school on Monday?"

They both smiled.

Jodi was outvoted again. But in the end, she couldn't help herself. She smiled, too. Their **fearlessness was contagious.**

And she was already trying to decide what she would build first.

Chapter 7

PART TREE! PART HOUSE!
PART RECYCLED MATERIAL!

Normally, Morgan loved weekends. But all he could think about now was getting back to Doc's goggles—and back into Minecraft.

He was able to play at home, without the goggles, of course. But his screen time was limited, and Po and Harper weren't available to join him for multiplayer. **He logged on for a bit and reviewed crafting recipes.** He even fought some zombies. It was all good practice.

They needed better gear in their shared VR game. Weapons and armor would keep them safe. He'd suggest it on Monday.

In the meantime, **he saw Minecraft**

everywhere he looked.

On Friday night, he went to the grocery store with his dad. In the cereal aisle, he crossed his eyes. The cereal boxes blurred. Now they looked like blocks of colorful ore. He saw **emerald and gold** and his favorite, lapis lazuli.

On Saturday morning, he helped his parents with yard work. Trees swayed in the breeze. He saw the trees as green blocks stacked on top of brown blocks. He imagined all the things he could build with their wood: **a shield, a raft, an entire cabin.**

On Sunday afternoon, he felt his life force drain away as surely as if a venomous cave spider had poisoned him: Ash Kapoor was having a party. And as his sister kept reminding him, he was invited.

"It'll be fun," Jodi promised. "Ash is so nice. And our whole class will be there."

Morgan grumbled.

When he and Jodi arrived at Ash's house, they heard shrieks of laughter coming from the backyard. They followed a narrow sidewalk around the house and through an open gate.

Their entire class was there, just as Jodi had promised. Kids were climbing up, sliding down, and crawling all over a huge structure.

"What is that thing?" Morgan asked.

"It's a tree house!" Jodi answered. "It's the most glorious tree house I've ever seen!"

Morgan had to admit it was impressive. The tree house was big and colorful, with rope bridges and trapdoors, a big plastic slide, and turrets. Through the second-story window, Morgan could see cozy cushions and a bookshelf. It was like two playgrounds and a library all shoved together.

Po was in a tire swing. He waved madly at them as he swung past. Harper looked down on them from an upper level. She waved, too.

"Hey, come on up!" she called. **"You've got to see this view."**

Morgan and Jodi grinned at each other.

"Race you up," said Morgan.

"I'll go up the climbing wall!" said Jodi.

Jodi beat him to the top, but only by a few seconds.

Harper wasn't kidding. It was a great view. Ash's house was next to a big stretch of woods. The tree house looked out over a bright green canopy.

Morgan noticed **the letters QAV etched into the wood railing.** "What's that mean?" he asked. "Quite a view?"

"Quinn Alice Vega," said Ash. Morgan turned to see her standing close by.

"Quinn was a friend of mine back in California," Ash said. "She helped me make this platform and the railing. She said the best part about being in a tree house was being able to see for miles around." She paused for a second. **Morgan noticed she was absentmindedly rubbing the Carpentry badge on her scouting sash**. "Here. Follow me."

Morgan, Jodi, and Harper all followed her to the other end of the platform. She stood beside the door to the cozy reading room. She pointed to another set of initials ornately etched into the old doorframe: *LWE*.

"Luanne was a big reader. She said a tree house needed a space for books."

"Hold on," said Morgan. "You built this whole thing with your friends?"

Ash nodded. **"I built it with my Wildling Scouts troop** back in California. We all worked together. A little bit of each person's personality came out in the section they worked on the most."

"No wonder it's so great," Jodi said. "It's a house of friendship!"

"Also, it's very sturdy," said Harper. **She hopped up and down** and nodded her approval.

"That's a compliment, coming from her," whispered Jodi.

"But how did you move this thing all the way from California?" asked Harper.

Ash smirked. "It wasn't easy, but my parents found a way. When they told me we were moving again, I told them I refused to go with them.

I said we couldn't just leave the tree house behind, not after all the work I'd put into it. So my mom had some of her engineering friends take it apart, and they gave us instructions on how to put it back together."

"Sounds like a fun puzzle," said Harper. "Like the coolest jigsaw ever."

"That's pretty clever of your parents, too," said Jodi.

"Yeah," said Ash. Her voice was a little sad. "After that, they said, 'Now you have no good reason to want to stay in California.' As if my friends weren't a good reason."

Harper and Jodi both nodded. They were probably imagining what it would be like to move away and start over somewhere new.

For the first time, Morgan realized how difficult things must be for

Ash. **He understood a little better now—** even though he wasn't quite ready to welcome her with open arms. He was always afraid someone cooler than him would swoop in and take his friends. And at the moment, Ash seemed pretty cool.

He noticed Jodi making a weird face. She sort of scrunched up her nose and bit her lip while rocking on the balls of her feet.

Morgan knew that face. She was struggling not to say something. **She wanted to tell Ash about their Minecraft adventure!**

But Morgan had made her promise not to tell anyone about it, and he knew she would keep their secret.

Ash would be just fine on her own. They shouldn't feel sorry for her. She had this amazing tree house, after all. And when the class went home for the evening, she'd have the whole thing to herself. **How cool was that?**

Chapter 8

SPIDERS: DON'T CALL THEM INSECTS! DON'T CALL THEM FRIENDS!

Harper wondered if the VR goggles would work a second time. She still couldn't wrap her mind around the science of how they worked. **What if the whole adventure had been some strange dream?**

She met the others in the computer lab on Monday afternoon. Ms. Minerva was there, reading a book—the kids knew she loved science fiction and fantasy novels—in a little office off to the side. The teacher waved hello to Harper through the glass.

Doc Culpepper was nowhere to be seen. Harper thought their science teacher had probably already moved on to her next project. Most geniuses were like that—they didn't stand still for long.

But Harper could never leave a puzzle unsolved. And right now, these goggles were the biggest mystery around.

She held her breath and put on the goggles. There was a flash of light. And then she and her friends were back in the burrow. The bed, the torch, the crafting table, and the furnace were just where they'd left them.

"**COOL,**" Harper said.

"Way cooler than that tree house," Morgan said.

"**MORGAN, I'M TRYING TO STICK MY TONGUE OUT AT YOU,**" said Jodi. "**BUT I'M NOT SURE I HAVE A TONGUE HERE.**"

Harper dug a hole in the dirt wall. Daylight poured into the burrow.

"The sun's out," Po said. "**WE SHOULD GO EXPLORING.**"

"I agree," Harper said. "I want to see as much as possible. I want to figure this place out!"

"I ALREADY KNOW HOW THIS PLACE WORKS," Po said. "IT'S MAGIC."

Harper turned toward him. She was going to tell him she didn't believe in magic. But Po was gone. He had been replaced—with a wizard!

"WHO ARE YOU?" Harper asked. "WHAT DID YOU DO WITH PO?"

The wizard laughed—with Po's voice.

"IT'S ME," he said. "I JUST CHANGED MY SKIN. TA-DA! Want me to show you how?"

"NO, THANKS," Harper said. She looked down at her arms and hands. "This whole thing is strange enough. I'd like to stay . . . me."

"SUIT YOURSELF," said Po.

Harper stepped through the narrow opening,

and the others followed her outside. They climbed to the top of the hill. They couldn't see very far; the hill was surrounded by trees.

"**WHICH WAY SHOULD WE GO?**" asked Morgan.

"**I SUPPOSE IT DOESN'T MATTER,**" Harper said.

Po stroked his wizard's beard. "**AYE, FORSOOTH, THOU ART WISE. MAGIC IS IN THE JOURNEY, NOT THE DESTINATION.**"

Jodi giggled. "Po, why are you talking like that?"

"**I'M GETTING INTO CHARACTER!**" he said.

"I'd give you a thumbs-up," Jodi said, "but, well, you know . . ."

"**NO THUMBS,**" said Po.

"**I WISH I COULD MAKE A COMPASS,**" Harper said. "That way we could find our way back here. But I don't have the materials."

"**WE CAN JUST PACK UP THE BED AND TABLE AND FURNACE AND GO,**" Morgan said. "If we have the bed, we can exit and come back whenever we want."

"LET'S TAKE THE TORCH, TOO," Harper said. "Just in case."

"GOODBYE, BURROW," said Jodi. **"THANK YOU FOR KEEPING US SAFE FROM ALL THOSE ZOMBIES."**

"FORSOOTH!" said Po.

 As they walked, Harper picked up everything she could: Dirt. Flowers. Apples. She knew that anything might prove useful later.

"WHY ARE YOU DOING THAT?" Jodi asked when Harper picked up a sapling.

"THIS IS HOW I ALWAYS START A NEW GAME," Harper said. **"I GATHER AS MANY RESOURCES AS POSSIBLE."**

"I'VE NEVER PLAYED SURVIVAL MODE," Jodi admitted. "In Creative, you start with everything you need. And you also don't spend half your time hiding from monsters."

Harper said, **"EVENTUALLY WE'LL BE ABLE TO CRAFT WEAPONS. AND ARMOR.** We won't have to hide forever."

"BUT FOR NOW, LET'S BE CAREFUL," said Morgan. "Most hostile mobs spawn at night. But you never know. . . ."

"AND WE CAN'T BE SURE THAT THIS PLACE WORKS EXACTLY LIKE A NORMAL GAME OF MINECRAFT," Harper added. **"DOC KEPT MENTIONING GLITCHES."**

She saw a purple flower growing beneath a tree. It was a bit out of the way, so she hurried over to pick it up. But her hand passed right through it.

Jodi was watching. **"IS THAT A GLITCH?"** she asked.

"NO," Harper said. **"MY INVENTORY IS JUST FULL."** She walked back to rejoin the others. "It's the first lilac I've seen. But we don't really need it. Flowers are only good for making dyes."

"BUT I MIGHT WANT A PURPLE BED!" said Jodi. "Really purple."

"AND INDEED, SUCH DELICATE BEAUTY

IS A REWARD IN ITSELF," Po added in his smarmiest wizard voice.

"HUH?" said Jodi.

"HE SAID FLOWERS ARE PRETTY," said Harper.

"I'll grab it," Jodi said. **"I HAVE PLENTY OF INVENTORY SPACE."**

As Jodi stepped through the trees, Harper saw something strange. Red lights moved in the shadows beneath the trees. They almost looked like a car's brake lights. But there were no cars here.

"SPIDER!" Harper said. **"JODI, DON'T PANIC."**

Harper knew that a spider wouldn't attack unless it was attacked first. Unfortunately, Jodi didn't know that.

Jodi panicked. **She punched the spider,** and it flared with red light as it took damage. Then it turned its bright red eyes on her.

"NOW YOU'VE DONE IT," Morgan said. **"RUN FAST!"**

Jodi ran, and the spider followed.

Morgan hurried over and smacked it on the abdomen.

The spider flared red. Now it turned its eyes on Morgan.

"HARPER!" Morgan cried. **"WE NEED A SWORD!"**

"I'M WORKING ON IT!" Harper yelled. She double-clicked with her eyes to pull up her inventory. Everything was a mess—she hadn't had time to put things in any sort of order. "I need the crafting table," she said, passing her eyes over everything she'd collected. **"THERE! ONE SWORD, COMING UP."**

Once she'd placed the table, she selected two sticks and a wood plank.

Clunk.

She hadn't made a sword. She'd made a shovel.

"OOPS!" she said. **"I GOT THE RECIPE WRONG."**

"THAT WILL STILL WORK!" cried Morgan. **"I'M COMING YOUR WAY!"**

Morgan turned toward her. The spider was on

his tail.

"GET READY," he said.
Morgan passed her. The spider was just behind him. She swung the shovel.

The spider flared red. It flopped onto its back and disappeared in a puff of pixelated smoke.

"WHEW," Morgan said. **"I'M GLAD WE DON'T RUN OUT OF BREATH HERE."**

"Good job, team!" said Po. "Wait, I mean: **EVER DO THE BONDS OF FRIENDSHIP VANQUISH DARKEST EVIL!"**

"What did it drop?" Jodi said.

"SPIDER EYE," Harper said brightly. **"THAT MIGHT COME IN HANDY."** She reached for it but couldn't pick it up. It slipped right through her grasp. **"OH, RIGHT. MY INVENTORY IS STILL FULL."**

"You should hold on to that mighty shovel," said Jodi. **"AND I'LL CARRY ALL THE MATERIALS YOU WANT."** She frowned at the spider eye. **"EVEN THE GROSS ONES."**

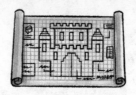

Chapter 9

MINING! CRAFTING! THIS IS WHAT IT'S ALL ABOUT

Po scanned the trees for any other dangers. All was still and silent.

"THAT SPIDER ALMOST GOT ME," Morgan said.

"AND ME," Jodi said. **"BUT WHAT WOULD IT HAVE DONE TO ME IF IT HAD CAUGHT ME?"**

"We don't know," Harper said. **"IF WE RUN OUT OF HEALTH HERE . . . WHAT HAPPENS TO US IN REAL LIFE?"**

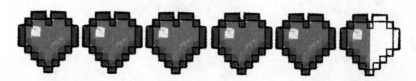

"I know you love to learn new things, Harper," said Po. **"BUT THAT IS ONE MYSTERY I'D RATHER NOT SOLVE."**

"I remember how to make a sword now," Harper said. **"MAYBE I SHOULD MAKE ONE. OR FOUR."**

Morgan pointed to her shovel. **"OR MAYBE YOU SHOULD MAKE A FEW OTHER TOOLS,"** he said. "Do you still have your pickaxe?"

"WHY?" asked Po. **"AREN'T SWORDS BETTER FOR FIGHTING MONSTERS?"**

"YES," said Morgan. "But other tools are better for digging. **AND I THINK IT'S TIME WE WENT UNDERGROUND."**

They discussed Morgan's plan during lunch the next day at school.

"We need to build a real shelter," he said. "It's the best way to defend against hostile mobs."

"A home base. That sounds like a fun project," Po said enthusiastically.

"Not just a home base," Morgan said. **"A castle."**

"We'll need a lot of materials," Harper said.

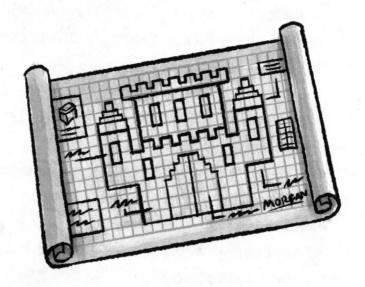

Morgan nodded. "Right. **I found a blueprint online, and a list of supplies.** For starters, we'll need eight hundred blocks of cobblestone. I'd like to get some glass panes for the windows, if we can find sand." He paused. "Wait. **Where's Jodi?** She was supposed to meet us here."

Po was the first to spot her. She was walking their way with a tray of food. And Ash Kapoor was with her.

"Hi, Ash!" Po said loudly. He said it to be polite . . . but also to warn Morgan. **Obviously, Doc's VR goggles were a big secret.**

Morgan scrambled to put the blueprint away, but he wasn't very sneaky about it. Ash gave him a funny look.

"Hi, everybody," Ash said. "Jodi invited me to sit with you. I hope that's okay."

"Sure," said Harper.

"Of course," Po said. **But he saw Morgan scowling.** He hoped Ash didn't; that wouldn't make her feel very welcome.

Morgan squirmed in his seat. "Jodi, did you forget? We were supposed to talk about our . . . project today."

"Oh, what kind of project?" Ash asked. "For school? Maybe I can help."

"No, it's . . ." Morgan hesitated. "It's like a secret after-school project."

"Oh. Okay," Ash said. She and Jodi were still standing there, holding their lunch trays. There was a moment of awkward silence.

Jodi rolled her eyes. "Fine," she said. "You guys have your meeting. Ash and I will sit over there and have a lovely lunch. Feel free to join us when you get tired of whispering secrets that don't even need to be kept secret."

Jodi stormed off, and Ash followed her. Morgan rolled his eyes. **Po thought doing things unexpectedly must run in the family.**

"Jodi's right," Po said. "We don't have to keep this a secret from everybody. We have two extra sets of goggles, remember?"

Morgan shook his head. "The more people who know a secret, **the less secret it is.** And if the adults find out we have a portal to an actual Minecraft world, I'm sure they'll take it away."

"It's not magical," Harper insisted. "It's science."

"Whatever. I just think we should keep

this between us for a little longer," Morgan said. "Deal?"

Po and Harper looked at each other. They were less certain. But they said, "Deal."

"Good," Morgan said. He pulled out his blueprint. "Now let's make a plan for tonight."

Chapter 10

TOO MANY COOKS! NOT ENOUGH COBBLESTONE!

"**WHO TOOK ALL THE OBSIDIAN?**" Jodi asked. She'd had it all set aside in a treasure chest. But now the chest was empty.

"**NOT ME,**" said Harper.

"**DON'T LOOK AT ME,**" said Morgan.

"**PO?**" Jodi asked.

"**HE'S NOT HERE YET,**" Morgan said. He sounded annoyed that Po was tardy.

They had been working on the castle all week. It wasn't going well.

"Wait a minute," Morgan said. "**WHAT DO YOU NEED OBSIDIAN FOR?** There's no obsidian in the plans."

"BUT IT LOOKS NICE," Jodi said. "And we don't have enough cobblestone. I thought we could replace some of it with obsidian. Maybe we could have a whole tower that's shiny and black." She closed her eyes and pictured it. "Oh, a black tower with diamonds like glittering stars! **WE CAN CALL IT THE NIGHT TOWER."**

Morgan hopped in frustration. **"WE DON'T HAVE TIME FOR STUFF LIKE THAT,"** he said. **"JUST FOLLOW THE BLUEPRINT, JODI."**

"I don't remember the blueprint." And she didn't—at least, not exactly.

That was one big problem with Morgan's plan: they couldn't bring

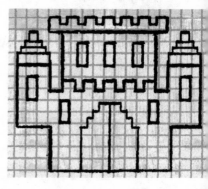

the blueprint into the game. Everyone tried to memorize the plans, but they all remembered the details a little differently.

"HARPER, WHAT ARE YOU WORKING ON?" Morgan asked.

She had been laying redstone dust along the

ground. **"I'M MAKING A SWITCH MECHANISM FOR THE DOOR,"** she replied.

"A switch?" Morgan said. **"IT'S A DOOR! IT DOESN'T NEED TO BE COMPLICATED."**

"BUT IT'S BETTER THIS WAY," Harper argued.

Morgan huffed. **"I SUPPOSE YOU DON'T REMEMBER THE BLUEPRINT, EITHER."**

"Oh, I remember it," Harper said. **"I'M JUST IMPROVING IT."**

There was a loud *pop,* and Po appeared nearby. At least, Jodi assumed it was Po. Today he'd chosen a skin that made him look like a construction worker.

"Hey!" he said. "What did I miss?"

"MORGAN IS HAVING A MELTDOWN," Jodi answered.

"Where have you been, Po?" Morgan asked.

"I TOLD YOU I HAD BASKETBALL PRACTICE," Po answered. **"I GOT HERE AS SOON AS I COULD."** He slapped his forehead. "But I forgot to look at the blueprint. I have no idea what I'm supposed to be building today."

"LET'S ALL JUST FOCUS ON MINING,"
Morgan said. "Okay? We need a lot more
cobblestone to finish the castle." He pointed at the
work in progress. So far, they had two gray towers.
These would become the castle's turrets.

**"IS THE NEW TURRET SHORTER THAN
THE OTHER ONE?"** Po asked. "Is that on
purpose?"

Morgan sighed.

**"MAYBE A CASTLE IS TOO DIFFICULT
FOR A FIRST PROJECT,"** Harper said. "We
have plenty of cobblestone for a nice cottage."

"I WON'T ADMIT DEFEAT," Morgan
said. **"NOT HERE. NOT IN MINECRAFT. I'M**

SUPPOSED TO BE GOOD AT MINECRAFT."

Jodi felt bad for her brother. He had his heart set on a castle. So she would help him make a castle. (Even if he didn't really deserve her help.)

"OKAY," she said. "BACK TO DIGGING FOR STONE." She raised her pickaxe high, then brought it down and struck the ground beneath her feet.

"NO, WAIT!" Morgan cried. But he was too late.

The pickaxe broke through the ground. And beneath it—there was nothing. Just blank black space.

Jodi fell.

Everyone screamed her name. Jodi screamed, too. But not for very long. She fell only the length of four blocks before landing on solid ground.

"I'M OKAY!" she said.

"What were you thinking?" Morgan said. She could see him above her, peering down into the hole. "YOU NEVER DIG STRAIGHT DOWN. THAT'S THE FIRST RULE OF MINECRAFT!"

"I thought there were no rules in Minecraft,"

Jodi argued. **"AND BESIDES, YOU CAN FLY IN CREATIVE MODE.** So this isn't usually a problem for me."

"YOU CAN FLY IN CREATIVE MODE?" Po asked. "Dude, Creative mode is sounding better and better."

Harper called down, **"YOU CAN GET YOURSELF OUT, JODI. JUST JUMP UP AND PLACE A BLOCK OF DIRT BENEATH YOUR FEET."**

Jodi did as Harper instructed. It didn't take her long to reach ground level. But when she did, she saw that the sun was low in the sky.

"GUYS, WE LOST TRACK OF TIME. IT WILL BE DARK SOON."

"And we're still not ready for any hostile mobs that might show up," Morgan said. **"WE'D BETTER HEAD INSIDE."**

They entered the nearest tower. It was partially built into a hill, so it was half underground. That made it bigger on the inside than it looked on the outside. Winding stairs led up to higher floors with windows.

"WHERE ARE THE BEDS?" asked Po, looking around the large underground room.

"WE PUT THEM IN THE OTHER TOWER," Jodi said brightly.

"THERE'S SUPPOSED TO BE A PASSAGE CONNECTING THE TOWERS," Morgan said. **"SO WE CAN GO BACK AND FORTH."**

"OOPS," Harper said. "I thought that was too boring. I was going to put in an automated mine cart instead. But I haven't had time."

Jodi put her ear to the door. "I don't hear anything out there. We could make a run for the other tower."

"NO, IT'S TOO RISKY," Morgan said. **"LET'S JUST TUNNEL THROUGH."**

Harper pointed to the far wall. **"THE HALLWAY IS SUPPOSED TO GO RIGHT OVER THERE."**

Morgan walked in the other direction. "I think this way will be more direct."

"I DON'T THINK WE SHOULD JUST TUNNEL THROUGH THE WALL," Harper said.

"Yeah, won't that direction take us through

the hill?" Po asked Morgan. "What if there's a mineshaft full of mobs on the other side?"

"IT'LL BE FINE," Morgan said.

Po and Harper looked at each other with slightly sour expressions. Jodi knew what they were thinking. This must have felt like their school science project all over again.

Morgan hefted his pickaxe. He removed two cobblestones and the dirt just behind them.

And then water gushed in through the opening.

They all screamed as the flood pushed them against the wall. The tower quickly began to fill with water.

"KEEP SWIMMING!" Morgan cried. "KEEP YOUR HEAD UP!"

They all swam over to the stairs and started climbing. They managed to stay above the rising water until they reached the top, where Harper broke through

the ceiling with her pickaxe. They exited through the hole she made.

Once they were safely on the roof, Harper sighed. **"I THINK WE'LL HAVE TO MAKE A BRIDGE TO THE OTHER TOWER.** I hope we have enough material."

Jodi pulled Morgan aside. **"THIS IS A DISASTER!** You keep insisting that we follow *you*. But when your teammates tell you not to do something, you do it anyway! What if that had been lava instead of water?"

Morgan frowned. "You're right. We got lucky. And this whole thing is a mess."

"FORTUNATELY, I HAVE A SOLUTION IN MIND," said Jodi. **"AND HER NAME IS ASH."**

"ASH?"

Jodi nodded. **"REMEMBER HER TREE HOUSE?** A whole group of scouts worked on it. Ash made sure all the pieces fit. If she can do that, she can help the four of us put a castle together."

"I DON'T THINK WE NEED HER HELP," Morgan snapped.

"WELL, I DO. AND I BET IF YOU PUT IT

TO A VOTE, IT WOULD BE THREE AGAINST ONE."

Morgan turned to watch Harper and Po. They were making a simple bridge to the other tower. One wrong move, and they would plummet all the way to the ground. At this height, who knew what the fall might do to them? **Jodi was in no hurry to find out what depleted health would mean in this version of the game.**

She knew exactly what her brother was thinking. He didn't want to bring Ash into their secret club. But he also understood that nothing was more important than the safety of their friends.

"ALL RIGHT," Morgan sighed. **"I'LL ASK ASH FOR HELP."**

Chapter 11

BARON SWEETCHEEKS IS LOOSE. AND HE'S NOT RETURNING MY CALLS!

Morgan grumbled all the way to Ash's house. But a promise was a promise. He would ask her if she wanted to join them for some Minecraft. He'd leave out the super-cool, possibly supernatural details. With any luck, the local Wildling Scouts would be keeping Ash too busy for another after-school activity.

He rang the doorbell. He waited only five seconds before deciding no one was home. He turned to walk away.

But then the door opened a crack. Ash peered at him from inside.

She looked . . . strange.

Her hair was all mussed. She had dust bunnies clinging to her clothing. There was a frantic gleam in her eyes.

"Morgan!" she said. "What are you doing here? Who sent you? What do you know?"

"Uh. Nothing?" said Morgan. **"Are you okay?"**

Ash didn't answer. Her lower lip quivered.

"Ash, what's going on?"

"If I tell you," she said, "do you promise not to freak out?"

Morgan was very confused. "Why would I freak out?"

"Because I've lost him," Ash replied.

"Who?"

"Baron Sweetcheeks has escaped!" Ash cried. She let out a huge breath, as if just telling someone had lifted a weight off her shoulders.

Morgan gasped at the news.

"I'm so sorry," said Ash. "I know how much Baron Sweetcheeks means to you. I'm going to find him. I'm sure of it."

"Let me help," said Morgan.

Ash looked at him with suspicion. "Really?" she said at last.

"Of course," said Morgan. **"Four eyes are better than two."**

Ash opened the door fully. "But I thought you hated me."

Morgan gasped again. *Hate* was such an ugly word. He had never hated anyone, ever.

"Why would you think that?" he asked.

Ash shrugged. "I kept trying to show you how much we have in common. Animals. Minecraft. And we both like spending time with Jodi. But you never seem to want me around."

Morgan felt awful. He knew he hadn't been very welcoming to her. **But he'd never meant to make her feel bad.**

He felt especially guilty because she'd been trying so hard to make a connection with him. To him it had seemed like she was trying to take his place, to show off, to be better than him at the things he loved. **But she'd only wanted to be friends.**

"Ash, I'm so sorry I made you feel that way," he said. "You're right. **We do have a lot in common.** And we both want to make sure Baron Sweetcheeks is safe." He held out his hand. "What do you say? **Hamster-hunting partners?**"

Ash smiled. She shook his hand. "Partners," she said. Then the smile disappeared from her face. "But I've looked everywhere. Where could he be?"

Putting himself in Ash's shoes had helped Morgan realize he'd been hurtful to her. Maybe a similar trick would work with the baron.

"We just have to think like a hamster," he said. "If you were a hamster . . . where would you want to go if you got loose?" Morgan tapped his chin. "Hamsters love food. . . ."

"I checked the kitchen, including all the cupboards," said Ash. "And my parents don't allow food anywhere else in the house."

"Maybe he got thirsty," Morgan suggested.

Ash shook her head. "There's a full bottle of water in his cage. I already looked in the bathroom. I even checked all the basement pipes for any leaks."

"The baron likes to have fun," Morgan said. "I built a little jungle gym for him to play in when I bring him home on the weekends."

"I don't have a hamster jungle gym," Ash said. She looked sullen for a moment. Then her eyes lit up. "Wait a minute! I do have something like that! Follow me."

Morgan followed Ash through her house. All

the cushions were on the floor, and the chairs had been tipped over. She'd clearly looked everywhere for Baron Sweetcheeks.

Everywhere but the backyard.

Ash opened the back door. Morgan was once again struck by how cool her tree house was. Of course that was where Baron Sweetcheeks would go! It was a perfect, gigantic playground for an active hamster.

Out of the corner of his eye, Morgan saw a flash of orange-brown fur on the tree house's upper level. **"There!"** he said, pointing. But the hamster was too quick. He lost sight of him.

"No, over there!" said Ash. "He's at the top of the slide!"

Baron Sweetcheeks slid into view then— literally! **The little furball slid headfirst down the slide,** his legs outstretched and his eyes wide. Morgan couldn't tell if the hamster was terrified or having the time of his life. Maybe it was both.

As soon as the hamster was at the bottom, he turned around and climbed up the slide to do it all over again. **His tiny nails clicked and clacked the whole way up.**

Ash started laughing. At first it was just a little giggle. Then she made a snorting sound.

That set Morgan off. Between Ash's snorts and the sight of the hamster coming down the slide again—backward, this time—he couldn't hold in his own laughter. It erupted from him like baking soda and vinegar from an overstuffed volcano.

When their laughter finally calmed down, Morgan wiped tears from his eyes. **"Are you free after school on Monday?"** he asked her.

"Sure," said Ash, wiping her own eyes. "Why?"

"Jodi and I want to hang out with you," he answered. "Po and Harper, too." He grinned at her. "And if you like Minecraft, you're going to love what we have to show you."

Chapter 12

REINTRODUCING: ASH! AVATAR OF EXPLORATION! HERALD OF TEAMWORK! TOTAL NOOB!

Ash was slightly nervous on her way to the computer lab. **Morgan had been very secretive** about what she would find there. And when she had asked Jodi about it at recess, Jodi had made a face like she might explode.

"I can't tell you!" Jodi had whispered . . . loudly. "I mean, I can! **It's not a secret from you anymore.** But it's way cooler if you see it for yourself!"

But what if Morgan had changed his mind? What if he'd decided he didn't want Ash around, after all?

Ash's worries disappeared the moment she

entered the room. Morgan was there to greet her. And not just Morgan. Jodi, Harper, and Po all looked happy to see her. Even Ms. Minerva gave her a little wave from behind the windows of the office.

"We're so glad you're here, Ash," said Harper.

"Yeah!" said Jodi. "Morgan, do you want to show her the blueprint?"

Morgan took a large sheet of paper from his backpack. It had an outline of a castle on it. He had made a lot of handwritten notes and what looked like directions along the edges.

Morgan stared at the paper for a moment. Then he seemed to make a decision.

He crumpled up the paper.

"You know what?" he said. "Let's just wing it."

"Wow!" said Jodi. "Really?"

"Wing it?" Ash echoed. "Wing what? What is the blueprint for?"

Po turned his wheelchair toward her. **"We're**

a sort of after-school Minecraft club. Our first project together is to build a castle."

"I thought the best way to do that would be to follow a design," Morgan said. "I like having instructions to follow. But sometimes I forget that not everyone feels the same way."

"A building project should be fun," said Po.

"And challenging," said Harper. "I'd rather make something new. **Something inventive.**"

"And I want it to be striking," said Jodi. "Like a work of art."

"Okay," said Ash. She gripped her chin. She nodded, and paced a little. "So you all agree that you want a castle. **You just disagree about . . . everything else.**"

Morgan gulped. "Is it hopeless? Should we make four separate castles?"

Ash stopped pacing.

"Just because it's challenging doesn't mean it's hopeless," she replied. "My scouting troop went through the same thing when we made our tree house."

"Really?" said Po. "But your tree house turned

out totally amazing."

"**And we did that by having a plan,** but also by letting each person bring their personality and skills to their task," said Ash. "Even if that meant the final product would be a little unusual."

"I can live with unusual," Morgan said. "We need our castle to keep us safe from **hostile mobs.**"

"Secure. Inventive. Fun. And striking." Ash nodded again. "We can do this." She smiled. "People say there's no *I* in *team*. But here's a secret: **the best teams allow you to stay true to yourself.**"

"I like that!" Jodi said. "What if there's been a silent *I* in *team* all along?"

Morgan looked through the office windows, where Ms. Minerva was reading a fantasy novel and drinking a cup of coffee. "Just don't try it on a spelling test," he said. **"But I'll try things your way, Ash."**

Harper patted him on the shoulder. "He's learning," she said, and everyone laughed.

"So should we get started?" said Ash. "Which monitor should I use?"

"Oh man," Po said. "I almost forgot. **This is the best part!**" He shared a smile with the others. Ash wasn't sure how she should react.

Po took a headset from a peg on the wall. Ash thought it looked strange—high-tech, but also a little bit otherworldly. It seemed to glow even though it wasn't plugged in to anything.

He handed it to her. **"Ready to give this a try?"** he said, still smiling.

"I have no idea," Ash answered.

"Trust us," said Jodi. "You're ready."

"Welcome to Minecraft," said Po.

"Well, yeah," Ash said, confused.

"The VR goggles make this a little different from the Minecraft you're probably used to," Morgan explained through a wide grin.

"Way different," Po said. He waggled his eyebrows and plugged in the headset.

Morgan laughed. "All right, Ash. Time to take your official VR goggles for a spin."

Ash nodded. She put on the headset.

It was dark for a moment, and then there was a flash of light.

And suddenly Minecraft spread out before her.

And above her.

And over her.

"HOW?" she cried in awe. **"WHAT—WHAT IS THIS?"**

Jodi appeared beside her with a *pop.* It was a

weirdly blocky version of Jodi, as if she'd been turned into a Minecraft skin. But it was definitely her.

"DON'T WORRY," she said. "IT SEEMS STRANGE AT FIRST. BUT THAT'S ONLY BECAUSE IT IS STRANGE."

"We're right here with you," said Harper.

"AYE, MY LADY, YE HAVE NAUGHT TO FEAR," said a knight in shining armor.

Ash laughed. Despite the helmet hiding his face, she knew it had to be Po.

"IS THIS COOL?" said Morgan. "OR IS THIS COOL?"

"IT'S INCREDIBLE," said Ash. "It's beautiful." She pointed at the two nearby towers. "ALTHOUGH THAT IS ONE SAD-LOOKING CASTLE."

They all laughed.

"Yeah," Morgan said. "WE'RE HOPING YOU CAN HELP WITH THAT."

Ash walked up to one of the blocky towers. **"I SHOULD TAKE A CLOSER LOOK,"** she said. She reached for the door.

"NO, WAIT!" Morgan said.

But Morgan's warning came too late. A flood poured from the door. Ash shrieked in surprise. The water pushed her back several squares.

Once the initial shock had passed, Ash took a wobbly step toward the group. **"IS THAT NORMAL?"**

"NOTHING'S REALLY NORMAL HERE," Morgan said. **"BUT DON'T WORRY. YOU'LL GET USED TO IT IN NO TIME."**

Chapter 13

YOUR HOME IS YOUR CASTLE! YOUR CASTLE IS YOUR HOME!

odi had been right. With Ash helping them, they finally made real progress on the castle.

And more important, they all had fun doing it.

They spent the first few days **making a mineshaft.** They were all nervous about it. But Ash insisted they needed more material to work

with. She reminded them to be careful.

So they dug. They placed torches every few squares. They set up doors in case they needed to retreat in a hurry. That way, anything scary they encountered wouldn't be able to follow them back to the surface.

A few times, **they heard strange sounds** in the depths. Those sounds were **proof of hostile mobs underground.** Whenever they heard something, they would put up a wall of dirt, turn around, and dig in another direction. They all had swords now, but as Ash put it, why fight if they didn't have to?

It was a good strategy. It allowed them to bring a lot more building materials up to the surface. And that meant fewer arguments about who got to use what.

Over the following week, Harper went wild with the small amounts of redstone they found. **She made a switch for the main entrance,** and even a simple trapdoor in case an unwelcome mob ever made it past the moat.

Po found a use for all the flowers they'd gathered. He arranged them all over the castle: around the exterior wall, within the interior courtyard, and **even in little flower boxes up on the turrets.**

Morgan was in charge of the four main turrets. He made them all identical. But he let Jodi place different stained glass windows in each one.

There was a fifth tower, too. This one was obsidian and rose from the very center of the fortress. And it was all Jodi's. Whereas the castle turrets were straight, this tower was twisted like a spiral. At its top was a wide platform for stargazing. **The platform was surrounded with decorative arches.** It was certainly strange, but she thought it was beautiful, too.

As she was putting on the finishing touches, a thought occurred to her. **"DID WE EVER FIND OUT WHAT HAPPENED TO THAT CHEST FULL OF OBSIDIAN?"** she asked.

"I thought Po took it," Morgan said.

"A BASE KNAVE I WOULD BE TO STRAY SO FAR FROM THE RULES OF CHIVALRY!" Po said.

"WHAT?" said Jodi.

"He said he didn't take it," said Harper.

"THAT'S WEIRD." Jodi said. She wondered if they had finally found one of the glitches Doc had warned them about. She hoped all the obsidian wasn't glitchy. What if her obsidian tower disappeared one day?

After nearly two weeks of daily progress, **Jodi had just one more task to accomplish.** This was something she and Ash had been working on in secret.

One day, when the others were in the mineshaft, Ash took Jodi aside and said, "It's ready."

They snuck away to a hidden plot of land. It was **a sunny patch of ground** on the far side of a hill, set right against a lake. The others couldn't see it from the castle. That made it the perfect spot for a secret garden. Ash and Jodi had planted wheat seeds there a few days before.

Jodi said, **"YOU'RE RIGHT! THE WHEAT LOOKS READY TO HARVEST."**

But wheat wasn't the surprise they had in mind.

Jodi and Ash waited at the top of a hill. They watched from a distance as Morgan and the others emerged from the mineshaft.

"WHERE HAVE YOU TWO BEEN?" Morgan

called. **"WE FOUND SOME GREAT STUFF!"**

Jodi turned to Ash. "Are you ready?"

Ash nodded. **"YEP."**

They walked down the hill toward the others. They each held out a stalk of wheat.

Two sheep followed close behind them.

"OH WOW!" said Po. **"SHEEP!"**

"THEY'RE FOLLOWING THE WHEAT," Harper said. "That's brilliant! We'll never have to go looking for wool again."

"AND THIS WAY, MORGAN CAN HAVE SOME PETS TO CARE FOR WHEN WE'RE HERE," Jodi said as she approached them.

Ash handed Morgan the

wheat. **"WE KNOW YOU LIKE ANIMALS."**

Morgan beamed. **"THIS IS GREAT. THEY'RE SO CUTE!"**

Jodi handed him her wheat, as well. **"IT'S MY WAY OF SAYING THANKS FOR BEING A GOOD BROTHER**—the kind of brother who listens to his little sister. Sometimes," she said.

"AND I WANTED TO THANK YOU FOR BEING A FRIEND," said Ash. "Even if it took you a little while to get there."

"THANKS," said Morgan. **"BOTH OF YOU. I LOVE THEM. I'M GOING TO CALL THEM BEAU AND BEEP."** The sheep bleated. They closed in on Morgan. Their pixelated eyes were fixed on the wheat he held. **"UH. BUT MAYBE WE SHOULD MAKE A FENCE REAL QUICK."**

Chapter 14

A WARNING WRIT LARGE! A PROMISE OF DANGER IN DAYS AHEAD!

Morgan loved having sheep at the castle. Beau and Beep were the perfect addition to their home away from home. And he would never have thought of raising sheep. **There was no animal pen in the blueprint** he had been so determined to follow.

Every time he looked at the animals, he was grateful for his friends and his sister.

He had something for them, as well. One final decoration for the castle.

"TA-DA!" he said as he revealed his gift. It was a wooden pickaxe set in a frame. He'd hung it on the wall.

"Cool pickaxe, noble squire!" said Po.

"I am not your squire," Morgan grumbled. **"AND IT'S NOT JUST ANY PICKAXE. IT'S THE FIRST PICKAXE HARPER MADE. THE VERY FIRST TOOL ANY OF US MADE,** back on our very first day."

"IT'S PERFECT," said Harper.

"SO THAT'S IT?" Jodi asked. **"ARE WE REALLY DONE?"**

Ash grinned. "All that's left is to admire the view from the top of the night tower. **I'LL RACE YOU!"**

They all hurried as fast as they could to the top, laughing the whole way.

And it really was an incredible view. Even better than the view from Ash's tree house. It made Morgan remember the initials carved into the railing: QAV.

"YOUR FRIEND QUINN WOULD LOVE IT UP HERE," he said to Ash.

"Yeah, she would," Ash replied. "MAYBE ONE DAY SHE'LL SEE IT. BUT RIGHT NOW, I'M JUST HAPPY TO BE HERE WITH MY NEW FRIENDS."

"We're happy, too," said Jodi.

"The happiest," said Harper.

"FORSOOTH!" said Po.

Morgan nodded in agreement. But as he looked off into the distance, he saw something that seemed out of place.

"WHAT IS THAT?" he asked.

They all looked where he was pointing. There was a little sliver of shiny black peeking out above the farthest trees.

"I can't tell from this angle," Harper said. "WE NEED TO GET HIGHER."

They all pulled blocks from their inventories.

Granite and cobblestone, andesite and diorite. They piled it all up, one block at a time. It wasn't pretty, but it helped them get higher and higher, until . . .

"Oh. Wow," said Po.

"WHAT DOES IT MEAN?" asked Jodi.

"I DON'T KNOW," said Morgan. "But it is weirding me out."

Morgan knew he didn't have a spine in avatar form. He knew he couldn't feel the temperature. Despite knowing these things, he felt a chill run down his spine now.

There in the distance, written in gigantic letters of darkest obsidian, was **a warning.**

Chapter 15

COUNTING TO SIX: ITS IMPORTANCE CANNOT BE OVERSTATED AT THE END OF THIS BOOK!

"**I** have never seen anything like that before," Ash whispered **as they returned from the game.** She had removed her headset and placed it back on its peg. They were in the computer lab,

and Ms. Minerva was reading a book in her corner office.

"It must have been meant for us, though," said Harper. **"It was a warning."**

"Or a threat," said Po.

"It certainly explains what happened to my stash of obsidian," said Jodi.

"But . . . but that means . . ." Morgan faltered.

"That means there was someone else in there with us. Watching us. Maybe the whole time we were in there!"

"But how?" Jodi asked.

"Um, guys?" Ash said. **"Aren't there usually six headsets?"**

She pointed to the wall. The sixth headset had been there earlier.

Now it was missing. The friends stared at each other. **Someone had taken the headset.**

They all looked at each other with shock and worry. The friends instantly understood what this meant. **They weren't the only ones who could enter the world of Minecraft!**

MINECRAFT is a game about placing blocks and going on adventures. Build, play, and explore across infinitely generated worlds of mountains, caverns, oceans, jungles, and deserts. Defeat hordes of zombies, bake the cake of your dreams, venture to new dimensions, or build a skyscraper. What you do in Minecraft is up to you.

Nick Eliopulos is a writer who lives in Brooklyn (as many writers do). He likes to spend half his free time reading and the other half gaming. He cowrote the Adventurers Guild series with his best friend and works as a narrative designer for a small video game studio. After all these years, Endermen still give him the creeps.

Luke Flowers is an author/illustrator living in Colorado Springs with his wife and three children. He is grateful to have had the opportunity to illustrate forty-five books since 2014, when he began his lifelong dream of illustrating children's books. Luke has also written and illustrated a best-selling book series called *Moby Shinobi.* When he's not illustrating in his creative cave, he enjoys performing puppetry, playing basketball, and going on adventures with his family.